Bear
Sees
COLORS

Karma Wilson

Illustrations by
Jane Chapman

SCHOLASTIC INC.

Mouse and Bear are walking;
they are chitter-chatter-talking.
So much for them to do.
And the bear

sees . . .

blue!

Blue flowers
by the trail.
Blue berries.
Blue pail.

Blue, blue EVERYWHERE!
Can you spy blue with Bear?

Along the trail hops Hare.
"Howdy-ho there, Mouse and Bear!"
Hare points up ahead.
And the bear

sees . . .

red!

Red blossoms.
Red cherries.
Red, juicy
raspberries.

Red, red EVERYWHERE!
Can you spy red with Bear?

Badger's at the pond
with his old galoshes on.
"Look there!" Badger bellows.
And the bear
sees . . .

yellow!

Drippy, sticky,
oh-so-yummy
honeycombs
with yellow honey.

Yellow, yellow EVERYWHERE!
Can you find it, just like Bear?

Gopher's out with Mole.
They are on a little stroll.
Bear spots them by the stream,
and the bear

sees . . .

green!

Green mint
for making tea.
Green and tasty
sweet peas.

Green, green EVERYWHERE!
Can you spy green with Bear?

Raven, Owl, and Wren
lay a picnic in the glen.
The friends all gather round,
and the friends

see . . .

brown!

Chocolate cake,
brown and sweet.
Brown cookies,
such a treat.

Brown eyes,
brown hair.
Friendly, fluffy,
brown . . .

BEAR!

Colors, colors EVERYWHERE?
Can you find colors, just like Bear?

To Emma. Bear and I say thanks.
—K. W.

To Jo, Jeremy, and Charlotte.
—J. C.

ISBN 978-0-545-80704-3

12 11 10 9 8 7 6 5 4 3 2 1   14 15 16 17 18 19/0

Printed in Malaysia   108

First Scholastic printing, September 2014

Book design by Lauren Rille
The text for this book is set in Adobe Caslon.
The illustrations for this book are rendered in acrylic paint.